Yogi Bear

BY S. QUENTIN HYATT

PICTURES BY M. KAWAGUCHI AND BOB BARRITT

GOLDEN PRESS · NEW YORK

As his many television admirers know, Yogi Bear's favorite food is honey. They may not be aware, however, that Yogi is also a sporting bear. In this amusing Little Golden Book adventure, Yogi brings fame and glory to the Jellystone Athletic team.

"Games! Fireworks! Ice Cream and Cakes!"
All the animals in Jellystone Park came to see the
notice on the News Tree.

"Come on, Boo Boo," said Yogi Bear to his friend.
"Let's go and join the Jellystone Team."

"Let's just eat ice cream and cakes," said Boo Boo. "It's easier and more fun."

"Why Boo Boo!" said Yogi. "At a time like this, Jellystone needs us. Besides, didn't I ever tell you that I was Rock Tossing and Boulder Lifting champion at Bruin University?"

"Yes Yogi, many times, but—"

"Come on," said Yogi. "I'll race you down to the glen. Ready, get set, go!"

Half way down to the glen Yogi stopped suddenly, then disappeared into the bushes.

"Yogi, Yogi, where are you?" called Boo Boo. "The glen is this way."

He found Yogi staring up at a tree.

"Look, Boo Boo," he said. "A lovely hive full of honey. Excuse me a minute."

"No, NO, Yogi," said Boo Boo. "Athletes are not supposed to eat honey."

"But honey is *good* for bears," muttered Yogi as he turned sadly away.

Coach Wiggins looked at Yogi, and he said, "H'mm." Then he said, "We'll be glad to have you on the team, Yogi, but you must practice hard. And remember, no honey-eating until the games are over."

"Honey is *good* for bears," said Yogi.

But Coach Wiggins wasn't listening.

For the next two weeks Yogi did his exercises every
morning.

He did push-ups—

and pull-ups.

He practiced Boulder Lifting

and Rock Tossing.

"Watch me lift this boulder," he said to Boo Boo.
"Ugh, grunt, phew! It must be stuck."

Poor Yogi! His mind was not on his work. All he could think of was that hive full of honey.

Every night as he went home he passed the tree.
The hive was still there. Full of honey.
"Honey makes bears *strong,*" said Yogi.
"No, NO, Yogi," said Boo Boo. "Remember what
Coach Wiggins said. No honey-eating until all the
games are over."

At last came the day of the big games.

The Jellystone Band played, and the team sang loud and clear:

"Jellystone, we love your flowers and trees,

Jellystone, we love your birds and bees,

Jellystone, we love your streams and lakes,

Jellystone, let's win for heaven's sakes."

The games started. But where was Yogi?
Coach Wiggins was worried.

"Boo Boo, go and find Yogi," he said. "Boulder
Lifting is next on the list."

"Don't worry, Coach, I'll find him. I bet he's at
home, taking a nap. He loves his naps."

Boo Boo ran off lickety split for Yogi's house.

Thump, thump, thump, he went on the door.

But there was no answer.

Yogi was not at home.

Boo Boo ran to the swimming hole. No Yogi.

He searched the huckleberry patch. No Yogi.

Where could he be? Then suddenly Boo Boo remembered the honey hive.

Sure enough, that's where he found Yogi. He was fast asleep under the tree, with a happy smile on his face. The hive was empty.

"Yogi, Yogi, wake up!" shouted Boo Boo.

"Hurumph," said Yogi. "Is it morning already?"

"No, it isn't morning, it's afternoon, and the games have started, and Boulder Lifting is next. Hurry!" said Boo Boo.

When they got back to the green, Old Redwood was ahead by one point.

"I'm sorry, Coach," said Yogi. "I couldn't stand it any longer. I had to eat that honey. Now that I'm well fed and well rested, I'm ready and raring to go."

There were five different-sized boulders to lift.
Harold Bear, of the Old Redwood team, went first.
He lifted the first four boulders easily, but the fifth
one was too heavy.

Now it was Yogi's turn.

Yogi stepped up to the lifting line.

He lifted the first four boulders easily.

"Now for the big fella," he said.

"Ugh, grunt," he said, and lifted the boulder up over his head.

"Yogi Bear is the winner," said the referee.

The crowd cheered.

Now came the Rock Tossing. Each player had to toss five rocks, and the one who tossed the furthest would win.

Harold Bear threw the five rocks high and far.

"Very good tossing, Harold," said Yogi. "Now let's see what old Yogi can do."

Yogi threw the rocks high and far.

The crowd waited while the referee went to see whose rocks had gone further. Would Yogi win and save the day for Jellystone?

The referee came back and said, "It's a tie! Now each player will have to throw one more rock."

"Quick, Boo Boo, get me some honey," said Yogi. "I can't take any chances now. This Harold Bear is a very good rock tosser."

"I just happen to have some honey with me," said Boo Boo. "Here—and good luck."

Harold Bear threw his rock. It went higher and higher and further and further. The Old Redwood team cheered. The Jellystone team groaned.

Then Yogi stepped to the tossing line, still munching his honey.

He picked up his rock. Round and round went his arm, then the rock flew up, up, up, and away it sailed, right over the tall pine trees and out of sight.

"Yogi Bear, Winner!" shouted the referee.

"Hurray for Yogi! Hurray for Jellystone!" shouted the crowd.

Harold and Yogi Bear shook paws.

"That was a fine toss, Yogi," said Harold. "How did you do it?"

"Well, Harold," said Yogi, "I can give you a little hint about Rock Tossing and Boulder Lifting. The most important thing is to get lots of food and lots of sleep. And don't listen when they tell you not to eat honey. Honey is *good* for bears."

"Gosh, thanks Yogi," said Harold. "I'll have to remember that."

That night, Yogi and Boo Boo watched the fireworks as they ate their ice cream and cakes. Right at the end, a big rocket shot into the sky. It had a flag on it that said, YOGI BEAR OUR HERO.

"Boo Boo," said Yogi, "this reminds me of my old days at Bruin University. Did I ever tell you that I was Rock Tossing and Boulder Lifting champion?"

But there was no answer. Boo Boo had gone to get more ice cream and cake—honey cake.